Once upon a Christmas...

FIVE "I BELIEVE IN JESUS"
READ-ALOUD STORIES

WILLIAM R. GOETZ

Illustrated by Edward S. Gazsi

HORIZON BOOKS

3825 Hartzdale Drive, Camp Hill, PA 17011
www.cpi-horizon.com

ISBN: 0-88965-153-1

98 99 00 01 02   5 4 3 2 1

Unless otherwise indicated, Scripture taken from the
KING JAMES VERSION of the Bible,
or the author's paraphrase.

Table of Contents

Introduction

Picture the scene.

It's almost Christmas, and anticipation in your home is high. On the fourth Sunday in Advent, just before bedtime, you gather your family in the living room.

The Christmas tree lights are on. Soft carols play on the stereo and the delicious smell of hot chocolate pervades the room as you pull up some cushions and cuddle with your youngest on the sofa. Big brother and sister, along with Mom, complete the scene.

It's *Once upon a Christmas* story time!

As you read "The Candy Maker's Christmas Wish" the Holy Spirit is at work in the hearts of your children. When the tale ends and you are led to make an appropriate application, one of your precious children genuinely understands the need for a personal relationship with Christ. Under your sensitive guidance, she opens her heart to the Savior.*

Suddenly Christmas is even more wonderful than you ever dreamed it could be!

A trademark in every Ed Gazsi drawing is a little mouse.
Your children may enjoy searching for this tiny creature.

For more information on how to lead your child to Christ, see the "Note to Parents" at the end of the book.

The Candy Maker's Christmas Wish

It is believed that Christmas candy canes date back to the early seventeenth century. In about 1670, a choirmaster in Cologne, Germany, is said to have bent traditional white sugar sticks into canes to represent a shepherd's staff in an effort to hold the attention of small children during a lengthy Nativity service.

The practice caught on, and the use of candy canes during Christmas services spread throughout Europe.

The custom was imported to North America in the mid-1800s by German immigrants. The red stripes and bands were added around the turn of the century as were the traditional peppermint flavors.

While the complete history of the Christmas candy cane may never be fully known, its symbolism has been the basis of a variety of stories and at least one song. It is a unique means of sharing the message of the redemption provided by the Lord Jesus Christ.

__Note to Parents:__ Have a candy cane to give to each child as a special treat at the close of this story. Use one of the canes during your reading to demonstrate the "J" of "Jesus" and the shepherd's crook, as well as to point out the white part and the red stripes of the candy.

Once upon a Christmas, in a pretty little village in a country far away, there lived a wonderful candy maker.

The candies he made in his candy kitchen were so good that people came from miles around to buy his delicious treats. His chocolates had scrumptious centers and mouthwatering coatings, colorful decorations and unique flavors that were better than any other candy maker could make. His hard fruit candies, peppermints, gumdrops and caramels were the very best anyone had ever tasted. His toffees just melted in your mouth! His candies were won-der-ful!

When people asked the candy maker how it was that he could make such fantastic candies, he would just smile and lower his head. He wouldn't say anything, for the candy maker was very shy. He was so shy that he had never married and lived alone. It was not easy for him to talk to people. If people pressed him for an answer, he would just smile again and say, "It's my secret recipe" and nothing more.

Now the candy maker not only made good candies; he was a good man. He was very kindhearted, for he loved the Lord Jesus and wanted to please Him. The candy maker also loved children—especially poor children. He would often slip a special treat into the pocket of a boy or girl who did not have enough money to buy some of his delicious candies.

Because the candy maker loved the Lord Jesus and children, he wanted very much to tell them—especially the poor children—about the Lord. He wanted them to know that Jesus came from heaven to be born in a manger at Christmas. He wanted them to know that He grew up and went about doing good—helping and healing, teaching and blessing people.

And he especially wanted to tell the children about how the Lord Jesus Christ died on the cross to pay for their sins so they could be forgiven, could become God's children and someday go to heaven. But because he was so very shy, it was hard for the candy maker to talk to people, even children.

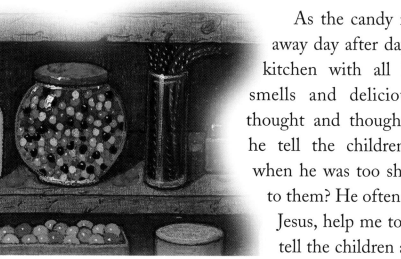

As the candy maker worked away day after day in his candy kitchen with all its wonderful smells and delicious treats, he thought and thought. How could he tell the children about Jesus when he was too shy even to talk to them? He often prayed, "Lord Jesus, help me to know how to tell the children about You."

As Christmas time came near, the candy maker wanted more than ever to tell people about the Lord Jesus. It was his dearest Christmas wish. And then one day, as he was making a fresh batch of Christmas candies, he had a wonderful idea! It was so wonderful that he knew at once it was an answer to his prayer.

As soon as he had finished the batch of Christmas candies, he set to work immediately on the idea. He worked and worked, and as he worked he smiled and smiled. Every now and then, he would burst into a happy song, for the candy maker was sure he had found a way to tell the children about the Lord Jesus.

About a week before Christmas, a large, neatly lettered sign appeared in the window of the candy shop. It read, "Free Christmas Candy! On Christmas Eve Day, every child who comes to the candy shop at 10 o'clock in the morning will receive a special gift of new candy." It was signed, "The Candy Maker."

The sign created a great deal of excitement. "New" candy—from the wonderful candy maker? And free? It sounded too good to be true.

Finally Christmas Eve Day arrived.

By 10 o'clock there was a large crowd of children jammed into the candy shop—so many that the parents had to wait outside in the cold! When the cuckoo clock cuckooed the hour, the candy maker came out of his kitchen carrying a very large box. He set it on the counter and then climbed up on a chair.

What the candy maker did next surprised everyone. He motioned for the children to be quiet and then he began to talk to them!

"Children," he said, "I want to give each of you a new Christmas candy which I have made. It's a candy that tells a story." He reached into his box and brought out a large candy that was white and red and shaped like a cane or a letter "J." He held it up high so everyone could see and said, "Before I hand out your candies, I want to show you how this candy tells a story."

When he said that, all of the children became very quiet and listened carefully.

Holding the candy so that it looked like a "J," the candy maker said, "This candy can stand for the letter "J," which reminds us of Jesus, who was born on the first Christmas. He is the Son of God who came to be our Savior."

Turning the candy up the other way, the candy maker said, "Now it looks like a shepherd's crook. That reminds us that Jesus is the Good Shepherd who gave His life for the sheep. That's us. Like sheep, we've all gone our own way. We've done bad things and deserve to be punished for our sin.

"But Jesus didn't want us to be punished. That's why He came at Christmas."

The candy maker then pointed to the white part of the candy.

"Jesus came to take away our sin and to make us pure and clean so that we can go to heaven. The red marks on the candy remind us of how the Lord Jesus takes away our sin. He did it by dying on the cross so we would not have to be punished and so that God can forgive us."

Pointing to the thin red stripes on the candy, the candy maker said, "These stripes stand for the stripes that Jesus took in our place when He was whipped and beaten just before He was crucified. The wide red stripes," he said, pointing to them, "remind us that Jesus shed His blood to wash away our sin. Now, when we are sorry for our sin and ask Jesus to forgive us and wash away all our wrong, He will do that and make us clean and ready for heaven."

The candy maker stopped talking then and just looked around at all the listening children. He smiled.

"I want to give each of you your candy now. I hope that, as you enjoy it, you will remember what it can tell us about the Lord Jesus. Most of all, I pray that you will ask the Lord to forgive your sin and be your Savior. Merry Christmas!"

What a happy time that was as each child got a big Christmas candy cane! And how happy the candy maker was! His dearest Christmas wish had come true. He had found a way to tell the children about the Lord Jesus Christ.

I'm quite sure that some of them did ask the Lord to be their Savior and that none of them ever forgot the lessons of the Christmas candy cane.

I hope you will also learn them, and ask Jesus to be your Savior too.

The Man Who
Missed Christmas

Once upon a Christmas there was a busy man named Greg Johns who lived in the big city of New York.

One of the reasons that Mr. Johns was so busy was that it was near Christmas—always a hectic time. This year his department was busier than usual, however, because the company was having a huge new safe put into the office.

On top of that, the people in the office were getting excited about Christmas. The holiday bustle was in the air.

But Mr. Johns was *not* excited about Christmas. In fact, he didn't want anything to do with what he called the "Christmas spirit." Something had happened years before, when he was still a boy, that had made him a bitter person—especially about Christmas.

Mr. Johns' unhappiness had also made him a lonely person. Somehow he didn't seem to be able to become a real friend with anyone. He lived alone and tried to find happiness by working very hard, getting ahead and making lots of money.

He did make lots of money and became an important vice president in the large company where he worked. But Mr. Johns wasn't very happy.

Some of the people in Mr. Johns' office were Christians who truly loved the Lord Jesus. They could see that even though Mr. Johns was

a vice president and made a lot of money, he didn't have a happy or peaceful heart. They wanted him to get to know the Lord Jesus.

Occasionally one or another of these Christians would invite Mr. Johns to a meal at their home or to come with them to a special musical event or service at their church. But he always said, "No."

Finally, after one invitation, Mr. Johns became quite angry. He said he'd heard what preachers say and what churches teach. He knew all about it and he didn't want anything to do with it!

But when Christmas drew near, Mr. Brown, one of the Christians, decided to try once again to just be a friend to Mr. Johns. He invited him to join the Brown family for Christmas dinner.

Again Mr. Johns said, "No!" His plans for Christmas Day were to relax. He would eat out at a nice restaurant.* "I'll be just fine, thanks," he said.

*If your children know that the restaurants in your area close
on Christmas Day, explain that such is not the case in New York City.

And so the day before Christmas arrived. At three o'clock in the afternoon, the office closed and the employees left early for the holiday.

Mr. Johns, as usual, stayed after everyone else left, because he had an especially important job to do. He had to put the company papers in the new safe which had finally been installed just that week.

The safe was very large—the kind people can walk into. Mr. Johns didn't know much about its operation, but Jim Roberts, the office manager, told him that he would set the lock so that all Mr. Johns would need to do when he was finished would be to close the door. "Then it will be time-locked until the morning after Christmas," Jim said.

Mr. Johns finished his work about 6:30 p.m., cleared his desk and went over to the safe to store the papers.

A few moments after he walked into the safe, something strange happened! The huge door slowly swung shut and closed with a loud click! The lights went out. He was trapped! Now what would Mr. Johns do?

As he stood there in the total darkness, he could feel his heart pounding. *How can I get out of here?* he thought frantically. Then he remembered what Jim had said: When the door closed it would be locked until the morning after Christmas!

Mr. Johns became even more frightened. Would he be able to

live until the door was unlocked or would he run out of air? He real-
ized that no one would miss him or come looking for him, since he
lived alone and had turned down a Christmas dinner invitation. What
would happen to him?

After a few minutes he felt his way carefully over to one side of the
safe, sat down and leaned against the wall. That's how he spent
Christmas Eve—sitting in the safe in the inky darkness, worrying
about having enough air to breathe.

That's how he spent most of the night, though he did occasionally
doze off to a fitful, restless sleep.

That's how he spent Christmas Day too. And the next night—worrying, hungry and thirsty, sleeping briefly, uncomfortable, tired and
bored. Nothing to do but think—and worry. He hadn't wanted to celebrate Christmas, but this certainly wasn't the way to spend a holiday,
either!

On the morning after Christmas, Jim Roberts was the first to come
into the office. With the time lock expired, he opened the door of the

safe. He didn't look in, but instead
went immediately to another part
of the building to attend to some
work.

Mr. Johns got up from his
cramped position and, blinking in
the light, stumbled out of the safe.
Without being seen by anyone, he
made his way unsteadily over to
the water fountain where he had a
long, long drink. Then he went out
into the street, hailed a taxi and
ordered the driver to take him to
his apartment.

After taking a shower, he prepared a simple meal and then slept for several hours. Awaking, he thought for a long time about what had happened to him. Finally, he shrugged his shoulders, got up, got dressed and went back to the office.

He had missed Christmas! And nobody had missed him!

But Mr. Johns didn't miss Christmas because he was locked in a safe. He missed Christmas because he chose not to know and love the Christ of Christmas, the Lord Jesus.

Many people miss Christmas, even though they celebrate with parties, decorations and gifts, but they have no place in their heart or home for the Lord Jesus Christ, the Savior.

Only when we have asked Jesus—the Savior born at Christmas—to be *our* Savior, can we really celebrate Christmas as God planned we should.

The Christmas Eve Storm

Once upon a Christmas there was a family who lived near a small town in the western part of the country.

They were a very nice family, with a father, Richard Moore; a mother, Kathy, and three children—John, eleven years old, Kathy, ten, and little Ricky, who was seven years old.

The Moores were a happy family—except for one big problem.

Mother and all three children truly loved the Lord Jesus and had asked Him to be their Savior. But Richard was not a Christian. He hardly ever even went to church with his family—except once in a while for something special, if the children really begged him to come.

The reason, he said, was that he could not believe the things that someone must believe in order to be a Christian. And, he said, he wouldn't pretend to believe by going to church and acting religious.

Still, he was a kind husband and father. He didn't try to stop his wife and children from believing in the Lord or going to church. When Kathy had become a Christian shortly after they were married, Richard had been surprised but understanding. They had talked about it a great deal then—and Richard had finally said, "Kathy, that's all right for you. If believing in Jesus makes you happy—that's fine. But I don't believe. I can't accept that God would become a man and die. Why should He?"

And so it was agreed that Kathy and the children—when they came along—could be Christians, but Richard would not believe and refused to talk about it.

Richard loved Kathy and the children a great deal, and they loved him. He worked hard to provide a nice home for his family from the money he earned as a professor at a nearby college. He also developed a small farm, with a little barn, a couple of horses, several cats, a dog and some chickens.

So, although the Moore family was happy, Kathy and the children wanted very much for Richard to become a Christian. They often prayed earnestly that he would believe in Jesus.

When Christmas Eve came, they especially wanted Father to come along with them to the service at the church. But he said, "No. You go to your meeting. I'll wait till you get home and we can have a nice family time then."

So off Mother and the children went, just as a storm began. The wind came up; wet, heavy snow started falling. Soon the ground, which had been brown and bare, was covered with white.

Richard built a fire in the fireplace and settled down to read a book while he waited for his family to come home. It was a very pleasant room, warm and inviting in the glow from the fireplace and the beautiful Christmas tree with its lovely lights.

Suddenly Richard heard a thump against the large picture window. He looked up from his book just in time to hear another, and another, and then several more thumps. Something was hitting the window! What could it be?

He got up and was going over to see, when Thump! Thump!—he saw two birds fly against the glass. Richard soon discovered what was happening. A flock of small birds, trying to escape the storm, were attracted to the light from his window. As they tried to fly in, they crashed against the windowpane and, stunned, dropped to the ground below.

Richard could see them now. They were cute little birds, huddled and shivering in the snow, which was beginning to cover some of them.

He thought to himself, *If they stay there, they'll freeze to death.* He wondered what he could do, and said aloud: "If I could just get them into the barn, they'd be warm and safe."

So Richard put on his coat, hat and boots and went out into the storm. He trudged over to the barn, opened the door wide and switched on the lights. Then he stood in the shadows and watched to see if the little birds would come into the warm, lighted barn.

But they did not move. They just huddled and shivered where they were.

Richard thought, *Maybe I can shoo them in.* He went over to the little flock, but he could not get them to go into the barn. Each time he came near, they scattered and fluttered away a short distance, huddling

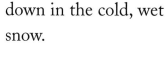
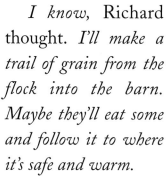

down in the cold, wet snow.

I know, Richard thought. *I'll make a trail of grain from the flock into the barn. Maybe they'll eat some and follow it to where it's safe and warm.*

So he quickly went into the barn, got a small pail and filled it with some of the grain he fed to the horses. He hurried back out into the storm and carefully scattered a trail of grain from the barn door over to where the flock was still huddling in the cold. But the birds did not move or pay any attention to the grain.

What can I do? worried Richard. *If it gets any colder they'll certainly freeze out here in the snow.* He thought and thought. Finally he said to himself, *If only I could talk to them. I'd tell them I don't want to frighten or hurt them. I'd tell them it's safe and warm in the barn.* Then he said aloud,

"If I could be a bird, I'd show them the way."

Suddenly, God caused Richard to understand in his heart that what *he* wanted to do for the birds was like what *God* did for people.

God had sent His Son, the Lord Jesus Christ, to become a man in order to tell us of God's love, and to show us that love by paying the penalty for our sins when He died on the cross. When Jesus was born as a tiny baby in Bethlehem, God was coming to live here as a Man who would take away the sin of the world.

Just then, as Richard stood in the falling snow, looking at the birds and thinking deep thoughts about God, the church bells in the town began ringing as the Christmas Eve service ended. "O Come, O Come, Immanuel," the bells were ringing.

And as he listened, Richard remembered Kathy telling him that the name Immanuel means "God with us."

He bowed his head and prayed, "Dear Lord Jesus, I believe. Please forgive me and be my Savior."

And in his heart, Richard had warm peace.

The Little Shepherd Girl

The idea of a shepherd girl is a new concept for many. It is presented as the result of recent research by Bible lands experts such as Rev. Ray Vander Laan, creator of the Focus on the Family Holy Land videos and Dr. Bryan Widbin, Professor of Old Testament at Alliance Theological Seminary. These and others indicate that many shepherds in Bible times were indeed young teen girls.

Once upon a Christmas long, long ago, there lived in Bethlehem a little shepherd girl named Leah. I want to tell you her story.

❄   ❄   ❄

Leah shivered as she sat down and leaned against a rock. She was tired and her hip hurt. She wondered how she was going to make it as a shepherd, for Leah walked with a limp.

When she was just a very small girl she had fallen down a steep hillside onto some rocks. Her hip had been badly hurt. Even after staying in bed for weeks, she had not been able to walk properly. In fact, she had never been able, ever since, to walk without limping and hurting.

"Leah the Limp" was what some of the mean kids called her. That hurt almost as much as the pain in her hip.

But she was older now. She would soon be twelve—old enough to help with the shepherding, even though she had a bad hip.

So this was her first year to be one of the family shepherds, out in the night, along with several of her older cousins—some of them boys, but mostly girls—and a few of the "traveling shepherds." They were older men who went from place to place hoping to be hired by the flock owners.

Both younger people and older people were needed to have the right group of shepherds. The tenderhearted girls were very good at caring for the lambs and injured sheep. The older boys and the men were especially needed in case a lion or wolf came sneaking around or robbers tried to steal some sheep.

Tonight they were out in the fields to the west of Bethlehem, since the harvest was over and the shepherds were allowed to graze their flocks in the farm lands. Until the harvest ended they were forced to take their flocks to the east of the village—out toward and even into the wilderness. This was better than the wilderness.

Now it was almost midnight. Leah liked this time—the middle of the night. The sheep were bedded down, the fire burned low and it was quiet—so still you felt you could almost hear the stars.

Sometimes at "middle night" Leah talked with her cousins. Sometimes she dozed off. But most often she just sat and thought. She thought over many of the things her father had taught her about God and the Holy Scriptures. Though most girls didn't get a chance to learn such things, she had. Because she was an only child, her father had made an exception. Leah had learned a lot of spiritual truth—especially about the Messiah. When He came, her father told her, He would rescue the people of Israel from their enemies and reign like a king.

Leah often thought that when the Messiah came He would not only save Israel but would also heal people. She wished He would come soon and heal her limp, and, of course, free them all from the cruelty of the Roman armies who had conquered them and now ruled their land of Judea.

Suddenly, Leah's thoughts vanished and she cried out. Without any warning, just above the shepherds there appeared a shining being! All around him was brilliant, shimmering white light, so bright it made the night lighter than the brightest noonday sun. Leah had never seen anything like it and the brilliance almost blinded her. She and all the shepherds were terrified!

"Don't be afraid!" the angel said. "Behold, I bring you good tidings of great joy which will be to all people. For there is born to you this day in the city of David a Savior, who is Christ the Lord.

"And this will be the sign to you: You will find the Babe wrapped in swaddling clothes, lying in a manger."*

Then, when it seemed that the sky couldn't get any brighter, it did! Suddenly there was a huge number of angels with the one who had talked to them. Leah could hardly imagine so many shining beings! It was awesome!

In beautiful voices that sounded like mighty thunder they praised God. "Glory to God in the highest," they said. "And on earth, peace, goodwill to men."

---

*Swaddling clothes are long strips of cloth wrapped around a baby like a blanket. A manger is a feeding trough for animals.

After a few minutes, the wonderful praises ended. The angels dis-appeared—back into heaven. When the bright light was gone it seemed darker than ever, and once again it was very still on the hillside.

But not for long. In a moment the shepherds all began excitedly and loudly talking: "Let's go to Bethlehem and see this Baby the angel told us about!" shouted one of the older boys.

"Yes! Let's go right away!" said another. One of the traveling shepherds wondered aloud, "The Messiah? Born in Bethlehem? I've got to see this!" The chatter of voices sounded like a barnyard full of chick-ens at feeding time.

Strangely, the sheep had not scattered or been frightened by the bright light and the loud praises. Already they were quietly bedding down again and going back to sleep.

And so, leaving one of the traveling men with the sheep, the whole crew hurried off to Bethlehem. Leah tried her best to keep up, but it was hard work in the dark and over the rough ground. Besides, her hip really hurt. But she was determined. The angel had said the Christ—the Messiah—was born, and with all her heart Leah wanted to see Him!

When they got to Bethlehem they went to an inn. Then, as the angel had directed them, they softly entered the stable behind the inn. It was a limestone cave where cattle were kept.

But tonight there were more than just cattle in the stable. A very young, tired-looking woman lay on some straw on the raised platform by the manger. Beside her sat her husband. And in the manger—all wrapped up in cloths—was the Baby!

The shepherds crowded around, looking on in wonder. Leah, arriving last, squirmed her way up close to the manger. As she looked down at the tiny form there, she remembered the angel's words: "Lying in a manger . . . a Savior . . . Christ the Lord."

Leah did not understand it, but in a wonderful way she began to feel all light and joyful inside. Somehow she knew that she was looking at the Messiah, and she felt like she wanted to sing!

"What is the Baby's name?" she softly asked the tired young mother.

"Jesus," the woman replied, "because the angel who told us He would be born said that He will save His people from their sins."*

When she heard the mother say that, Leah felt another thrill. She remembered once more the words of the angel out on the hillside. And so did the other shepherds, who now began talking all at once, telling the couple what had happened to them that night in the fields and why they had come to see the Baby. The mother, Mary, especially seemed to pay great attention to everything that was said.

---

*The name Jesus means "Savior."

During the excited talking, Leah watched the Baby. With all her heart she believed what the angel had said, and though she did not understand everything, she worshiped the tiny, newborn Messiah.

After a while, remembering their sheep, the shepherds began to file out of the stable. Once outside, they again started talking loudly, praising God for what He had told them and allowed them to see.

As they passed some of the houses, people looked out to see what all the noise and excitement was about. The shepherds, becoming more boisterous as they went, loudly and joyfully told anyone who asked, and many who didn't, what they had seen and heard. The people could hardly believe it.

Leah, her heart almost bursting with joy, gladly joined in the praises and telling about the Savior.

Then, all at once she noticed something—something marvelous! She was not limping! She didn't hurt! And in her heart, Leah knew that she would not limp ever again. For God, who had sent the world a Savior that night, had touched her and made her whole.

God's Trees

"God's Trees" is one version of an Appalachian folktale which has been told and retold for the better part of a century. I have seen a copy of a children's story book published in the 1920s which included yet another version of the story. Several generations of children have been blessed by the creativity of the unknown storyteller who first conceived the concept.

This version is a slight adaptation of the story recorded in the early 1960s by the husband-and-wife team of Bud and Myra Dean, who, with "Andy Accordion" (played by Bud), regularly created children's programming for the missionary radio station HCJB in Quito, Ecuador.

"God's Trees" has been a favorite in our own family, first consisting of five children, but now grown to include twelve grandchildren. My wife Joyce and I dramatized it by having her narrate the words of "Mother Tree" and each of the "little trees." Such readings led to the practice of Joyce being lovingly referred to by one of our sons-in-law as "Mrs. Tree"!

We also used the story each year over a thirteen-year period at the annual Festival of Choirs in the Sevenoaks Alliance Church, Abbotsford, British Columbia, where I was senior pastor for seventeen years. Because there were nine choirs involved—several of these comprised of children—we felt that the story of "God's Trees," which appealed so much to the children, was the best way to conclude the evening. When backed up by creative organ music, appropriate to the various parts of the story, it became a much-loved Christmas season tradition which all ages anticipated and appreciated.

Use your creativity to enjoy to the full this old tale with a clear salvation application!

Once upon a Christmas, long ago and far away, a forest of trees grew on a hillside; little ones and big ones, old ones and young ones, tall ones and short ones. All grew happily together.

When summer days came they laughed in the warm sunshine and found life good. When the spring rains splashed on their shiny leaves they laughed too, for the rain was cool and silvery and lovely. When the first autumn days caused their leaves to turn to red and gold, they rejoiced in the gorgeous display of color. And when winter sometimes wrapped a blanket of snow around their bare limbs, they found life more beautiful than ever in the white, glistening stillness.

The trees were very happy with their life on the hillside. But sometimes they spoke of changes that would come, and—just as children do—they talked of things they would like to do and be when they grew up.

One little tree said, "You know, I should like to be a baby's cradle. Often I have seen people coming into the forest and some come carrying babies in their arms. I think a baby is the sweetest thing I have ever seen. When I am older I should like to be made into a bed for a baby."

A second tree spoke. "That would not please me at all. I should like to be something more important than that. I think I should like to be a great ship and cross many waters. I should like to be large and strong and stately. I should like to be loaded with costly cargo: gold and silver and precious stones."

Mother Tree grew troubled. "Pride," she said, "is a dangerous thing. I do hope your wish will not bring you sorrow."

One little tree stood off by himself, in deep reflection, but he did not speak.

"What would you like to be?" asked Mother Tree. "Have you no dreams for the future?"

"No dreams," he said, "except to stand on the hillside and point to God. What could a tree do that is better than that?"

Mother Tree looked at him fondly. "What indeed?" she said.

Years passed and the trees grew up. One day some men came into the forest and cut down the first little tree.

"I wonder whether I shall be made into a baby's cradle now," he said. "I hope so. I have waited so long."

But the little tree was not made into a cradle. Instead he was hewn into rough pieces and carelessly put together to form a manger* in a stable in Bethlehem. The little tree was heartbroken.

"I do not like this at all," he wailed. "This is not what I planned to be—shoved into this dark place with no one to see me but the cattle."

But God, who loves little trees, said, "Wait! I will show you something." And He did.

> Now there were in the same country shepherds living out in the fields, keeping watch over their flocks by night.
>
> And behold! an angel of the Lord came upon them, and the glory of the Lord shone around them, and they were greatly afraid.
>
> Then the angel said to them, "Do not be afraid, for behold, I bring you good tidings of great joy which will be to all people. For there is born to you this day in the city of David, a Savior, who is Christ the Lord. And this will be the sign to you: You will find the Babe wrapped in swaddling clothes, lying in a manger."
>
> And suddenly there was with the angel a multitude of the heavenly host praising God and saying: "Glory to God in the highest, and on earth peace, good will to men."

---

*A manger is a feeding trough for animals.

So it was, when the angels had gone away from them into heaven, that the shepherds said to one another, "Let us go now to Bethlehem and see this thing which has come to pass, which the Lord has made known to us."

And they came with haste and found Mary and Joseph, and the Babe lying in a manger. (LUKE 2:8-16)

Yes! It was our little tree that was now a manger. In the stillness of the night, God had come down, and the Baby who had been born to Mary was the Son of God.

The manger quivered with delight. "Oh, this is wonderful!" he whispered. "In all my dreams I never thought to hold a baby like this. This is better than all my planning. Why, I am part of a miracle!"

And out on the hillside, all the trees of the forest clapped their hands, because their brother, the little manger, had seen his wish come true.

❄   ❄   ❄

Many years passed by and again men came into the forest and cut down the second little tree.

I wonder if I shall be made into a great vessel now, he thought. *I have waited so long. Now perhaps I shall do the great things of which I have dreamed.*

But the little tree did not do great things. He was not made into a great vessel at all. He was made instead into a tiny fishing boat that fell into the hands of a simple Galilean fisherman named Peter. The little boat was most unhappy. One day he sat in the water beside the shore of Lake Gennesaret and pondered while Peter washed his nets.

To think that my life has come to this, he complained. *Just a fishing boat! And Peter is not even a good fisherman! He has toiled all night and taken nothing. It would have been better to have remained in the forest than to have come to this.*

But God, who loves little trees, said, "Wait. I'll show you something." And He did.

For out of the crowd came a person named Jesus, who entered into the little boat and sat down and taught the people. His words were words of such wisdom and beauty and power that the multitudes, and even the boat, listened with eagerness. When Jesus had finished speaking, He told Peter to launch out into the deep and let down his net again. And oh, there were so many fish—so many that the net started to break. The little boat trembled, not so much with the weight of the fish, as with the weight of wonder in his heart.

This is wonderful! he thought. *In all my dreams I never thought to carry a cargo like this. Why, I am part of a miracle! This is better than all my planning.*

❄   ❄   ❄

And out on the hillside all the trees of the forest clapped their hands because their brother, the boat, had found fulfillment.

The months went by and again men came into the forest and cut down the third little tree—the one that had wanted just to stand on a hill and point to God.

He was most unhappy. *I do not want to go into the valley,* he sadly thought. *Why couldn't men leave me alone?*

But men did not leave the little tree alone. They chopped it apart and put it together in the form of a crude cross.

The tree shivered. *Oh, this is terrible—they are going to hang someone on me! Oh, I never wanted this to happen to me. To think that I must take part in a crucifixion. I, who wanted only to point to God. This is awful!*

But God, who loves little trees said, "Wait. I will show you something." And He did.

For one day, outside Jerusalem, a great multitude gathered, and in their midst stood Jesus and beside Him was the cross. As they led Jesus away, someone grabbed the arm of Simon the Cyrenian, coming out of the country, and on him they laid the cross that he might carry it behind Jesus. And when they were come to a place called Calvary, there they crucified Him.

As the cross shuddered beneath its weight of agony and shame, suddenly a miracle happened. Jesus, when He had cried again with a loud voice, gave up His spirit and died.

And behold, the veil of the temple was torn in two from the top to the bottom. And the earth quaked, and the rocks split.

Then the centurion* and those who were with him watching Jesus saw the earthquake and the things that had happened, they feared greatly, saying, "Truly, this was the Son of God." (MATTHEW 27:51, 54)

The little tree that had become a cross heard floating down from heavenly places the echo of a remembered promise:

"Now is the judgment of this world, Now shall the prince of this world be cast out, and I, if I be lifted up from the earth, shall draw all men unto Me." (JOHN 12:31-32)

The cross began to understand. "This is wonderful," he said. "I'm part of a miracle! In all my dreams I never thought I'd point to God in this way. This is better than all my planning."

And so it was!

Hundreds of trees have stood on the hill slopes through the years, but not one has ever

*A centurion is a Roman soldier in charge of 100 men.

been able to point anyone to God. Only the cross of Calvary can do that.

And out on the hillside, all of the trees of the forest bowed their heads and thanked God, because their brother, the cross, had known fulfillment.

Just so, the three trees show us God's good news.

The first, the Cradle Tree, reminds us that God's Son came to earth at the first Christmas to be our Savior. The angel told Joseph and Mary that they were to call Mary's Son Jesus,* "for He shall save His people from their sins."

The Boat Tree helps us to remember that Jesus lived a sinless life. He never did a single wrong, but went about doing good—helping, loving, healing and blessing people.

The third tree, the Cross Tree, shows us how the Lord Jesus Christ died for our sins. He took the punishment that we deserve because we have sinned. Though He had never sinned and did not deserve to die, He took the penalty of death instead of us. Now, because He did, and then rose from the grave, we can be forgiven and free of the punishment God requires for sin if we will trust Him to be our own Savior.

---

*The name Jesus means "Savior."

Note to Parents

What greater joy can a parent have than that of leading his or her child to a personal knowledge of Jesus Christ as Savior and Lord?

This book is intended to help parents do just that.

Although leading one's child to Christ is an awesome privilege and responsibility, it is one which it is very possible to experience.

We know from history and personal experience that children have a great openness to spiritual things and to the Lord. As someone has said, "Children seem naturally able to open their hearts to God just as the petals of a flower open to the sun."

Statistics document this fact. According to Child Evangelism Fellowship (CEF), the vast majority of adult Christians became believers when they were children. The actual breakdown of age-related conversions cited by CEF International is most instructive:

PERCENTAGE OF ADULT CHRISTIANS WHO BECAME BELIEVERS AT:

Age	Percentage
0 - 4	1%
5 - 14	85%
15 - 30	10%
31 & up	4%

History also confirms this. The roll call of great Christians who were born again as "preschoolers" or young children is extensive. It includes such leaders as Count Nicolas Ludvig von Zinzendorf (1700-1760) who became the founder of that great missionary movement, the Moravians. Zinzendorf was converted at age six.

James Hudson Taylor (1832-1905) was converted and called to missionary service at age five, though it was not until age 17 that he had true assurance of salvation. Taylor founded the China Inland Mission.

The famed Chinese evangelist John Sung (1901-1949) was born again at age nine.

The founder of Bob Jones University, a powerful evangelist in his day, came to Christ and actually began to preach at a very early age.

David Wilkerson, of *The Cross and the Switchblade* fame, who came from a line of preachers, found Christ as a young child.

One of the best-known advocates for the Christian family in this century, Dr. James Dobson, founder of Focus on the Family, radio host, best-selling author and speaker, was introduced to the Savior by his father at age three!

As a five-year-old, I was led to trust Christ by my parents. They wisely utilized a teachable moment when I was painfully aware of the fact that I had disobeyed them (and thus God). I knew I was a sinner. Lovingly they helped me to clearly understand that I was lost and needed Christ. They encouraged me to repent and receive the Lord. I did, and I'm eternally grateful to them. Becoming a Christian as a child has spared me from a life of sin—with its costly consequences—and given me the privilege of serving the Lord all of my days.

What an incredible blessing—for me *and* my parents!

It's a blessing that all Christian parents should desire for their children and themselves. While care must be taken to avoid forcing the issue (pressing a child to make a decision which isn't motivated by a sincere desire, born out of the work of the Holy Spirit), an earnest parent will be prayerfully alert to the opportunity to guide his or her child to Christ.

It is our prayer that this volume may be a tool in the hands of the Holy Spirit to help create that priceless moment of opportunity for you with your child.

Though this book is intended primarily for use as a read-aloud resource for elementary school-age children, the stories can be adapted by any creative storytelling parent to the interests and age level of older or younger children.

Once upon a Christmas can be used by your family in a number of ways during the Christmas season.

One suggestion is to use the five stories as a part of your family's Advent celebration. That annual event in our family of five children was always a highlight. In a home in which there was no television and a tradition of reading stories aloud (even when the oldest were young teens), these occasions during Advent devotions were unquestionably a special treat.

The Advent season begins on the fourth Sunday before Christmas. On that day, in churches and homes, a wreath with four candles around the outside and one in the center becomes a focal point for family worship. One candle is lit the first Sunday and in each devotional time during that week. Two, three and then four candles are lighted in successive weeks. Then on Christmas Eve, with the four outer candles already lit, the youngest child in the family traditionally lights the center candle, which is symbolic of Christ, the Light of the world, and His incarnation in Bethlehem on the first Christmas.

One of the *Once upon a Christmas* stories could be read at each of the initial candle lightings as a special part of Advent. An alternate plan would be to read the five stories in succession on the five days leading up to and including Christmas Eve.

The stories could become part of a family's regular devotional time or be used individually with a younger child as a bedtime story. However, while these stories can be used anytime, it would seem best to use them in some special way which is tied to the Christmas event.

These stories are designed to teach the true message of Christmas—that Christ came to this world to save us. When the subject of salvation comes up, we have found it helpful to use what I call the "ABC Steps" (included at the end of this book) in explaining the gospel to children (and adults!). You may wish to consider a similar approach should your child be open to a salvation invitation. In doing so, it's important to adapt the biblical truth to the level of your child's comprehension.

It is essential that you earnestly call upon the Lord for your child's salvation and completely trust the Holy Spirit to guide you. The Spirit's guidance is essential in knowing the right time to "press" for a decision, the ability to clearly present the gospel and the wisdom to lead your precious child in a prayer of repentance, faith and invitation.

That is why, apart from the suggested "ABC's of Salvation" section at the close of the book, we have not attempted to provide a script for the act of introducing a child to Christ at the conclusion of each of the stories. We believe that parents can trust the Holy Spirit to provide the right transition to decision time at the opportune moment.

God bless you in your undertaking of this wonderful task.